BERNARD MOST

COCK-A-DOODLE-MOO!

RED WAGON BOOKS

HARCOURT BRACE & COMPANY

San Diego   New York   London

Red Wagon Books is a trademark of Harcourt Brace & Company.

Library of Congress Cataloging-in-Publication Data
Most, Bernard.
Cock-a-doodle-moo!/by Bernard Most.
p. cm.
"Red Wagon books."
Summary: When the rooster loses its voice and must ask the cow for
help to wake everybody, the resulting sound provides a hearty laugh
for the farmer and his animals.
ISBN 0-15-201252-4
[1. Roosters—Fiction. 2. Cows—Fiction.
3. Domestic Animals—Fiction.] I. Title.
PZ7.M8544Cm   1996
[E]—dc20   95-36097

First edition
A B C D E

Printed in Singapore

The illustrations in this book were done in Pantone Tria markers
on Bainbridge board 172, hot-press finish.
The display type was set in Antique Olive Bold and the text type
was set in Century Expanded by the Photocomposition Center,
Harcourt Brace & Company, San Diego, California.
Color separations by Bright Arts, Ltd., Singapore
Printed and bound by Tien Wah Press, Singapore
This book was printed with soya-based inks on Leykam recycled
paper, which contains more than 20 percent postconsumer waste and
has a total recycled content of at least 50 percent.
Production supervision by Warren Wallerstein and Pascha Gerlinger
Designed by Lori J. McThomas

The sun began to rise.
Time for the rooster to wake
everybody on the farm.

But when the rooster tried to make a loud COCK-A-DOODLE-DOO, only a whisper came out.

But the pigs slept on.

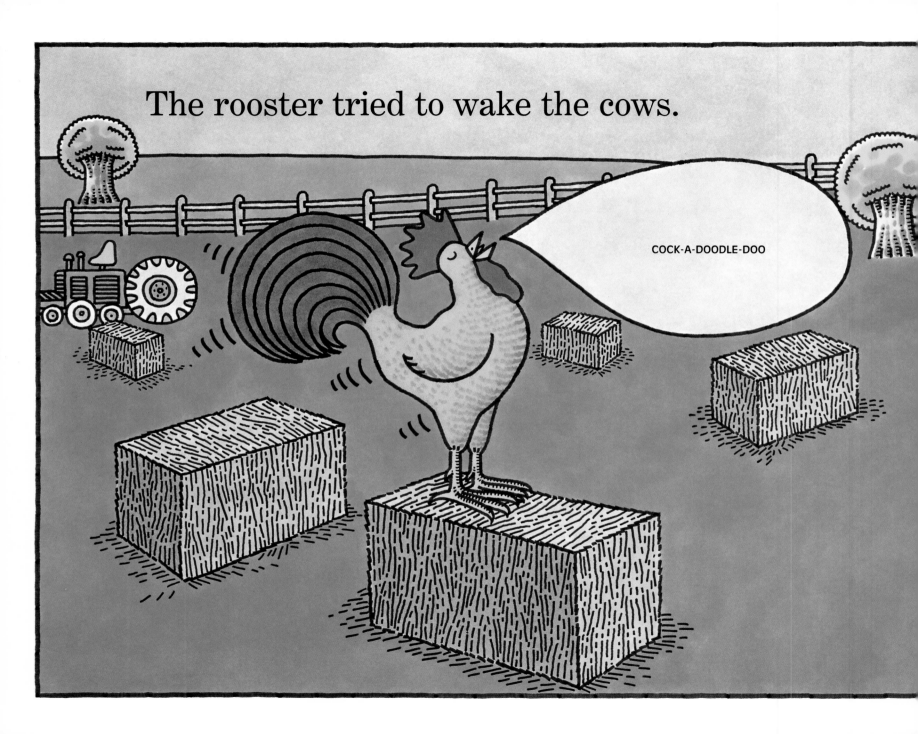

But the cows slept on.

The rooster tried to wake the ducks.

COCK-A-DOODLE-DOO

But the ducks slept on.

The rooster tried to wake the farmer.

Somebody had to wake the farm.
So the rooster tried
to wake the cow again.

The cow opened one eye.
She saw the rooster's problem.

The cow thought she could help.
Maybe she could go COCK-A-DOODLE-DOO.

The rooster wondered if he could teach
the cow how to go COCK-A-DOODLE-DOO.

COCK-A-DOODLE-MOO was close enough.

The cow went . . .

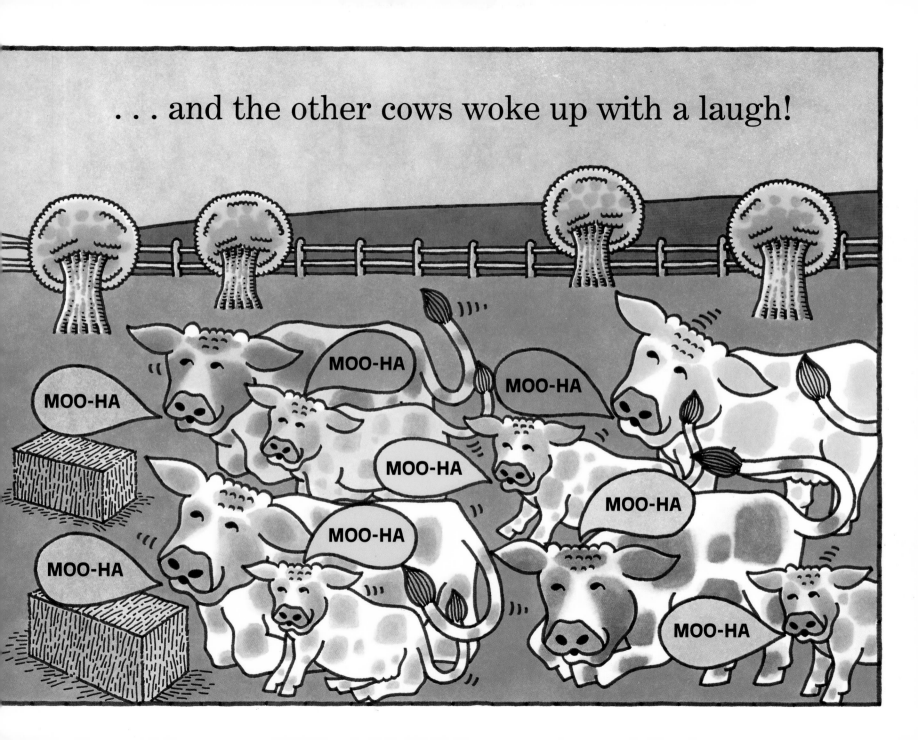

The cow went . . .

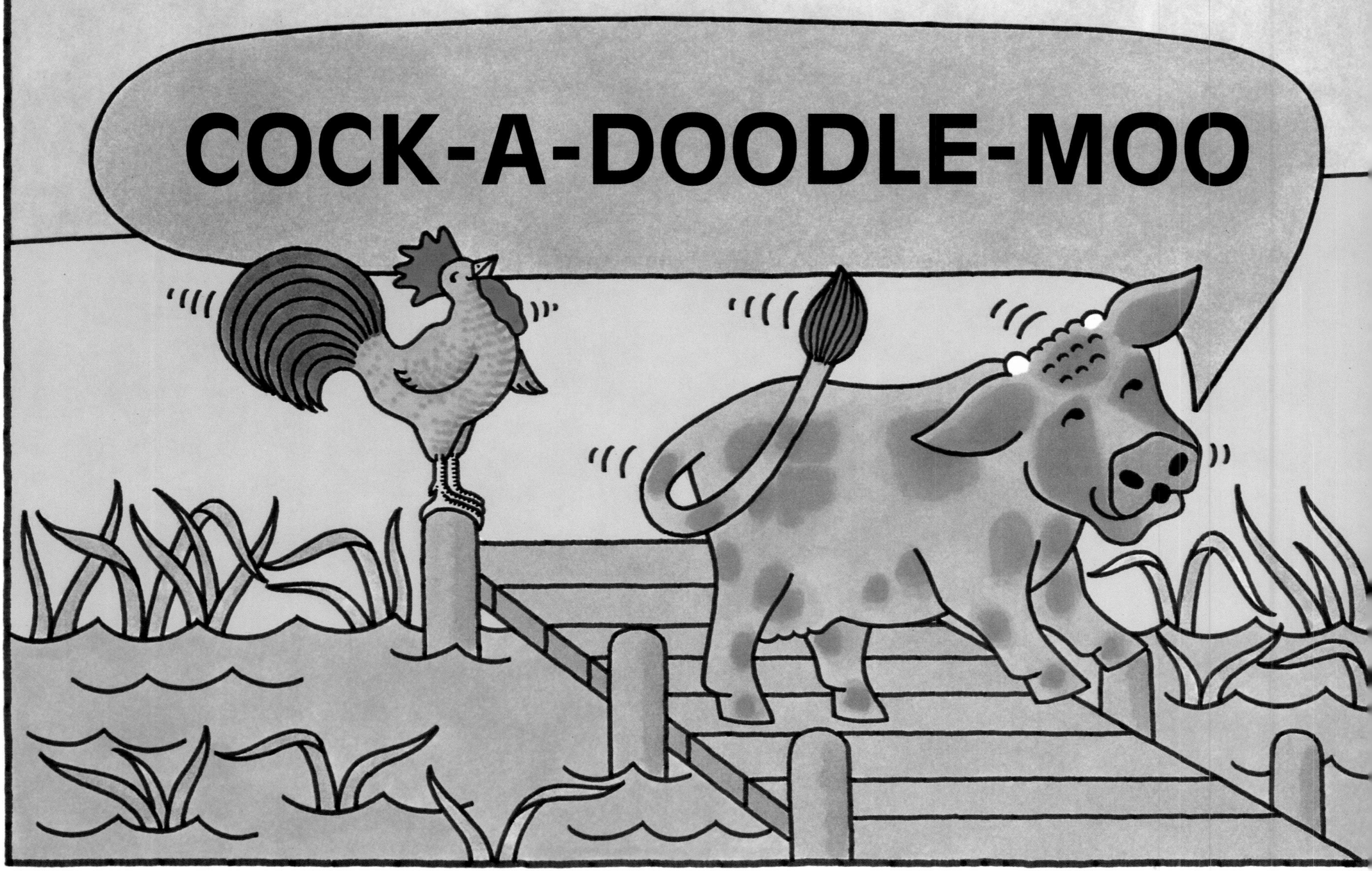

. . . and the ducks woke up with a laugh!

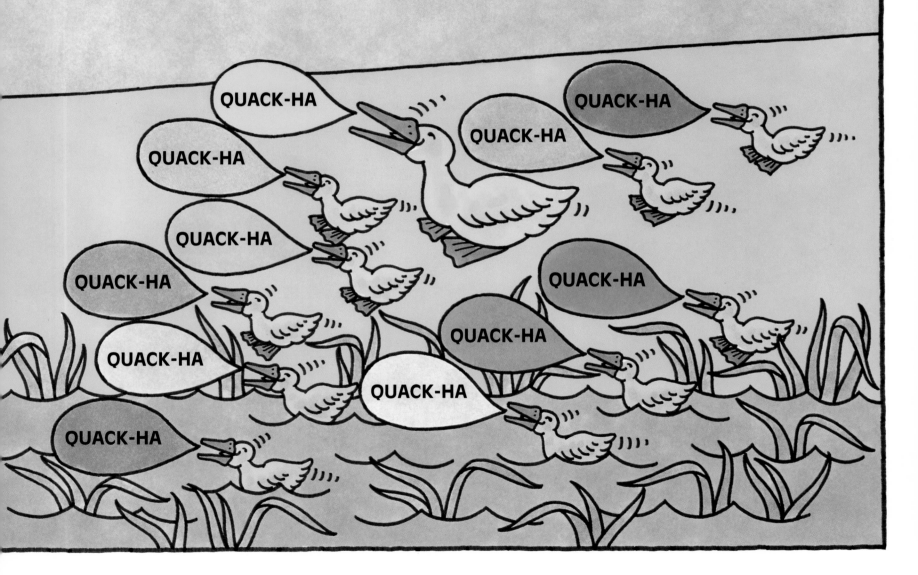

. . . the cow taught the rooster to COCK-A-DOODLE-MOO and they woke everyone on the farm together.